ACCLAIM FOR JEFF SMITH'S

Named an all time top ten graphic novel by **Time** *magazine.*

"As sweeping as the 'Lord of the Rings' cycle, but much funnier." **—Andrew Arnold, Time.com**

★*"This is first-class kid lit: exciting, funny, scary, and resonant enough that it will stick with readers for a long time."* **—Publishers Weekly,** *starred review*

"One of the best kids' comics ever." **—Vibe** *magazine*

*"***BONE** *is storytelling at its best, full of endearing, flawed characters whose adventures run the gamut from hilarious whimsy . . . to thrilling drama."* **—Entertainment Weekly**

"[This] sprawling, mythic comic is spectacular." **—SPIN** *magazine*

Rock Jaw
Master of the Eastern Border

OTHER **BONE** BOOKS

Out from Boneville

The Great Cow Race

Eyes of the Storm

The Dragonslayer

BONE

ROCK JAW
Master of the Eastern Border

BY JEFF SMITH
WITH COLOR BY STEVE HAMAKER

graphix

An Imprint of

SCHOLASTIC

New York   Toronto   London   Auckland   Sydney   Mexico City   New Delhi   Hong Kong   Buenos Aires

All rights reserved. Published by Graphix, an imprint of Scholastic Inc., *Publishers since 1920.* SCHOLASTIC, GRAPHIX, and associated logos are trademarks and/or registered trademarks of Scholastic Inc.

Library of Congress Catalog Card Number 95068403.

ISBN-13 978-0-439-70627-8 — ISBN-10 0-439-70627-0 (hardcover)

ISBN 0-439-70636-X (paperback)

ACKNOWLEDGMENTS

Harvestar Family Crest designed by Charles Vess

Map of *The Valley* by Mark Crilley

Color by Steve Hamaker

12 11   11 12/0

First Scholastic edition, February 2007

Book design by David Saylor

Printed in Singapore 46

This book is for Krishna and Avaday Iyer

CONTENTS

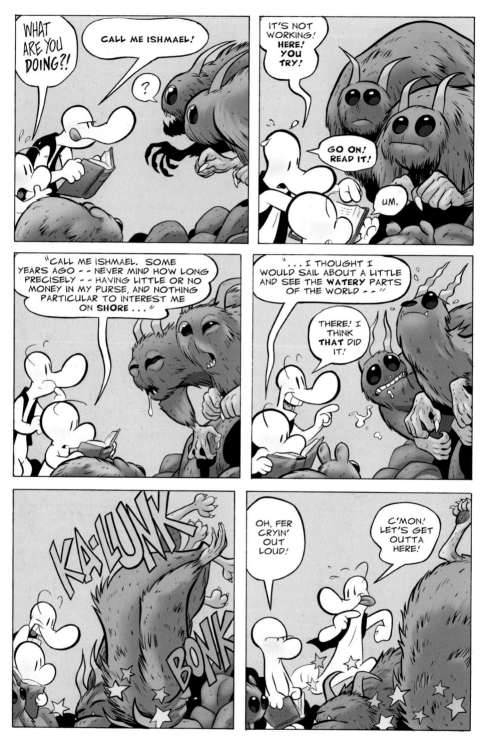

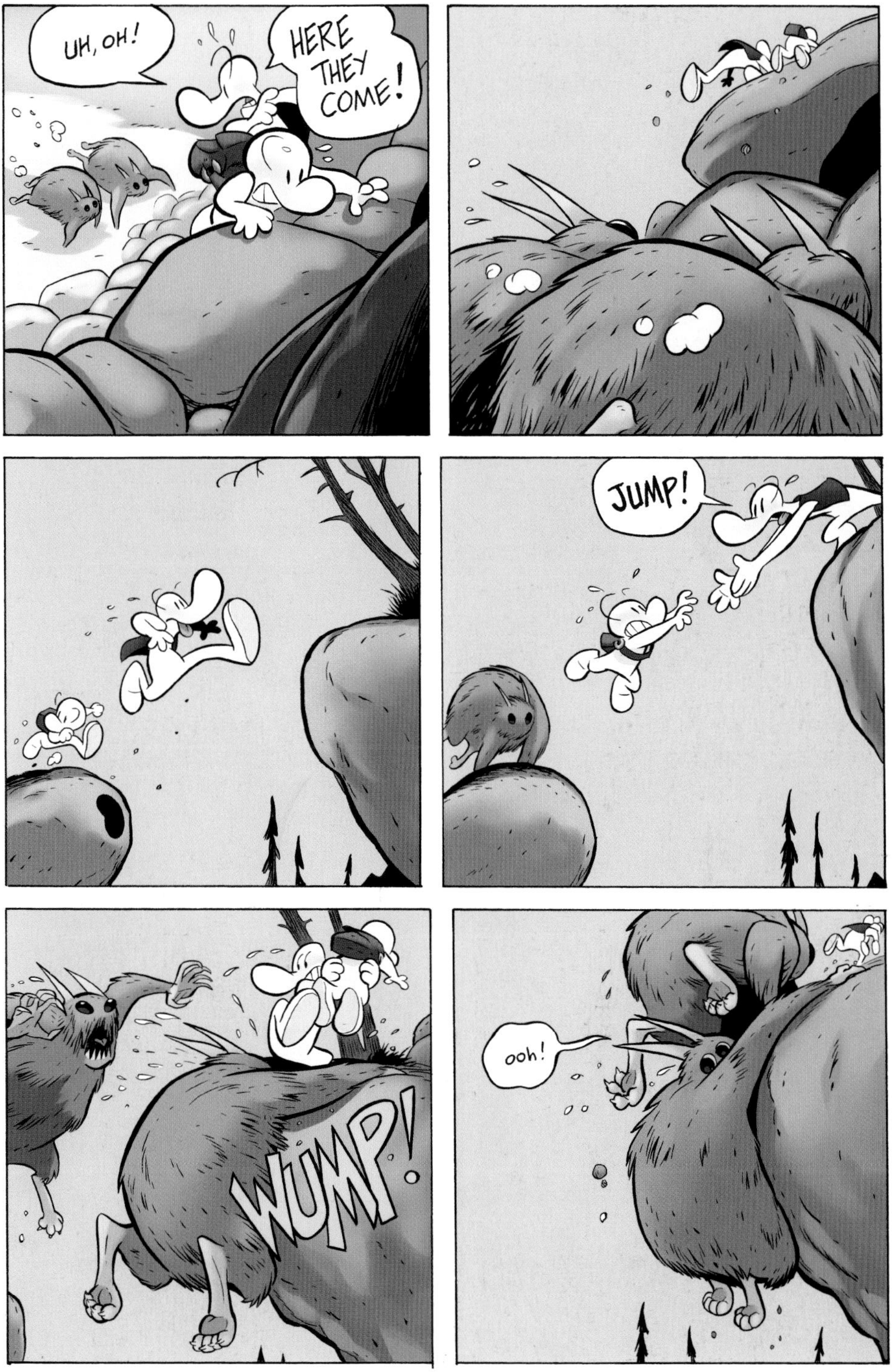
UH, OH!
HERE THEY COME!
JUMP!
WUMP!
ooh!

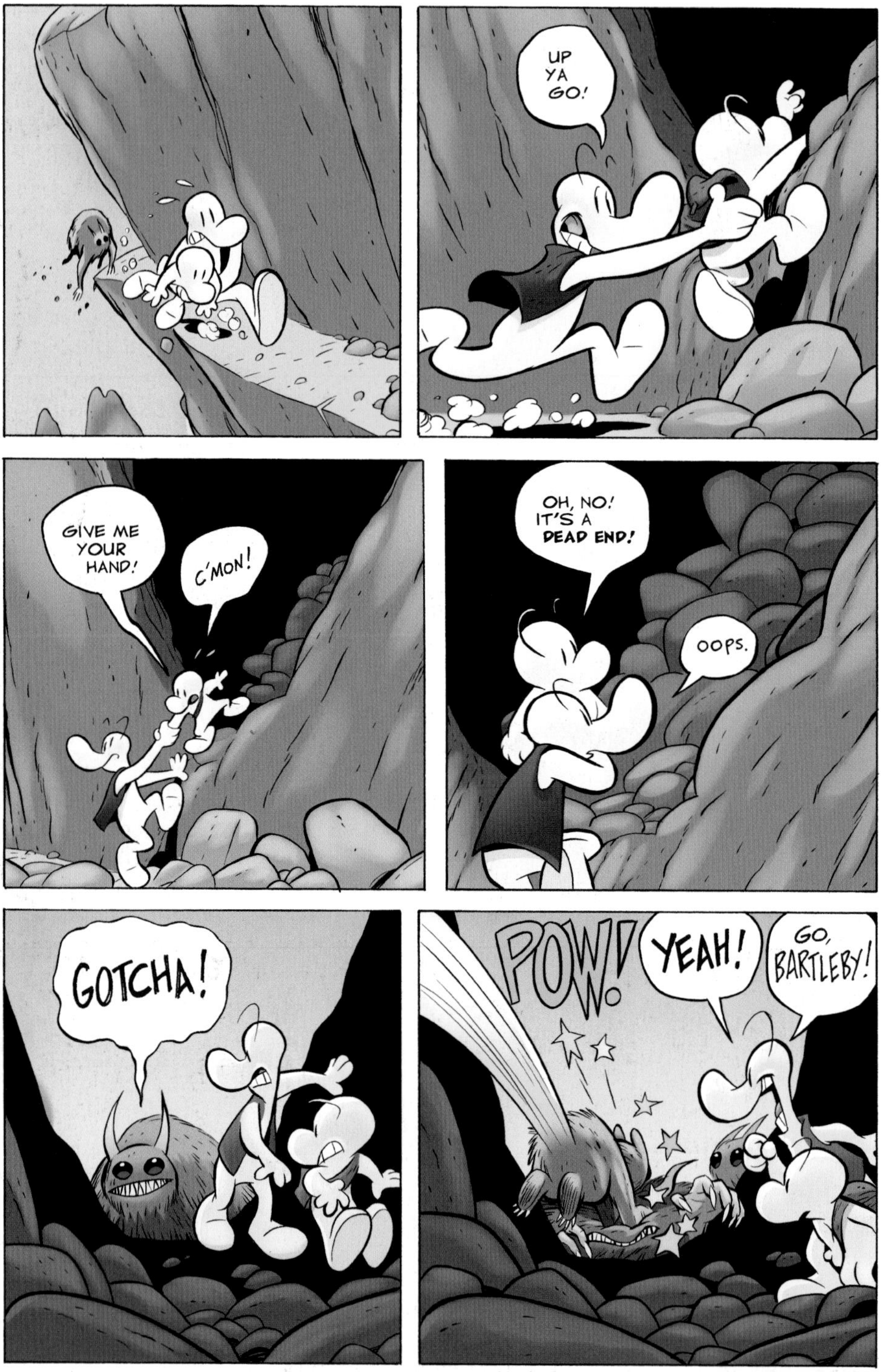
UP YA GO!
GIVE ME YOUR HAND!
C'MON!
OH, NO! IT'S A DEAD END!
OOPS.
GOTCHA!
POW!
YEAH!
GO, BARTLEBY!

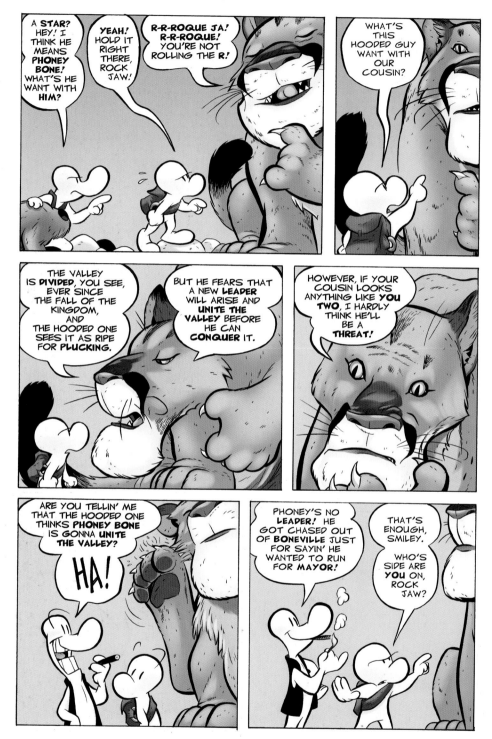

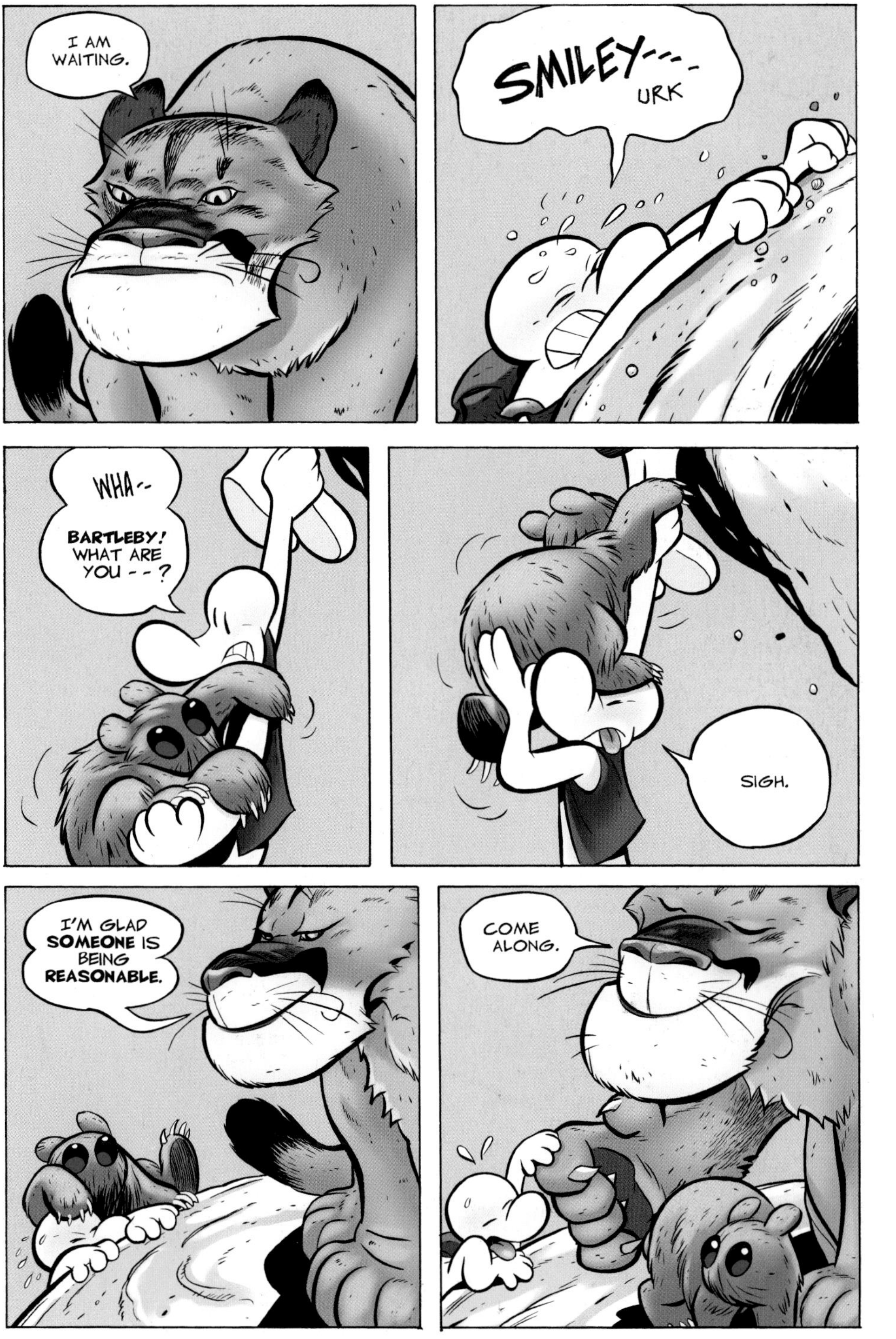
I AM WAITING.
SMILEY- - - -
URK
WHA- -
BARTLEBY! WHAT ARE YOU - - ?
SIGH.
I'M GLAD SOMEONE IS BEING REASONABLE.
COME ALONG.

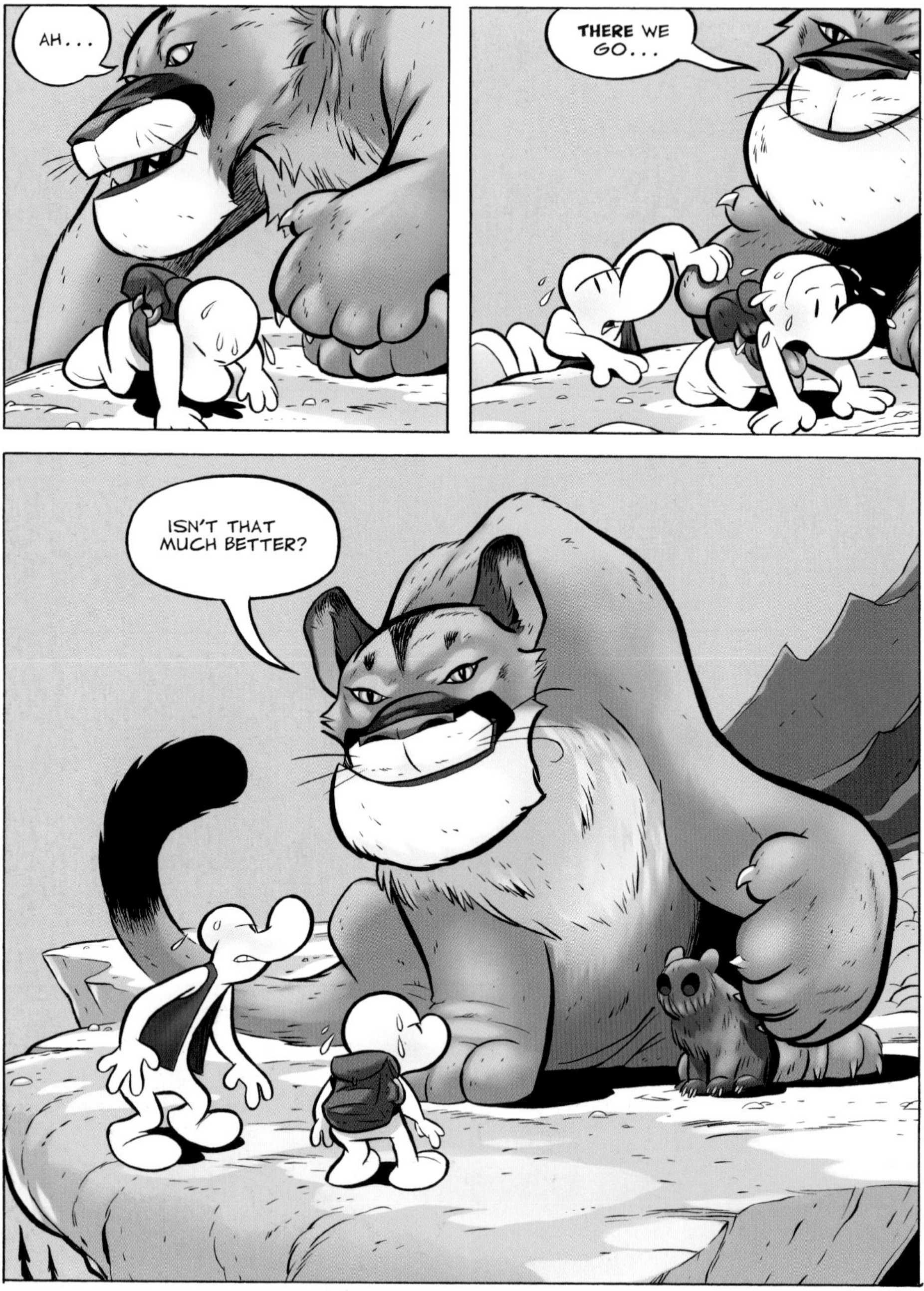
AH...
THERE WE GO...
ISN'T THAT MUCH BETTER?

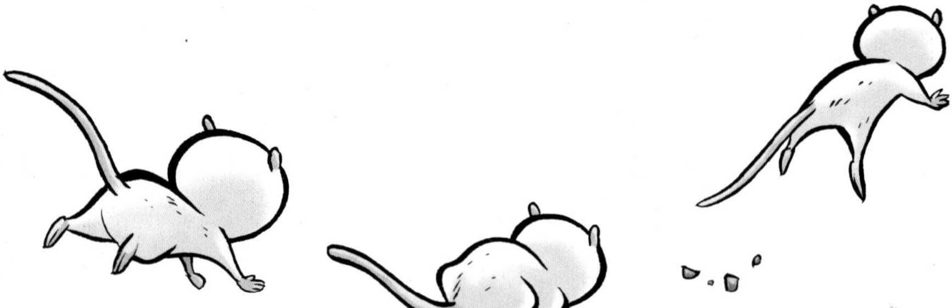

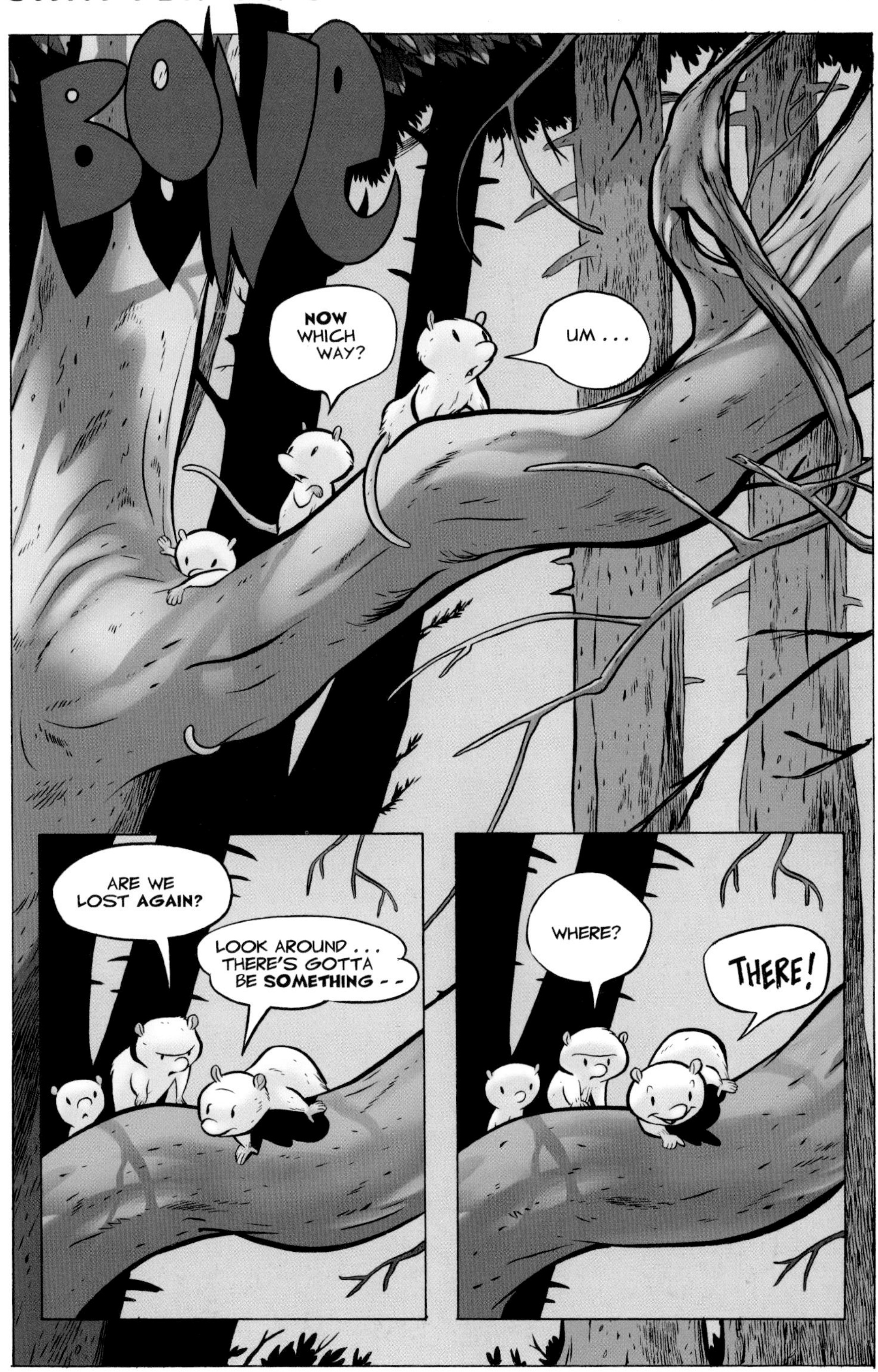
BONE
NOW WHICH WAY?
UM . . .
ARE WE LOST AGAIN?
LOOK AROUND . . . THERE'S GOTTA BE SOMETHING - -
WHERE?
THERE!

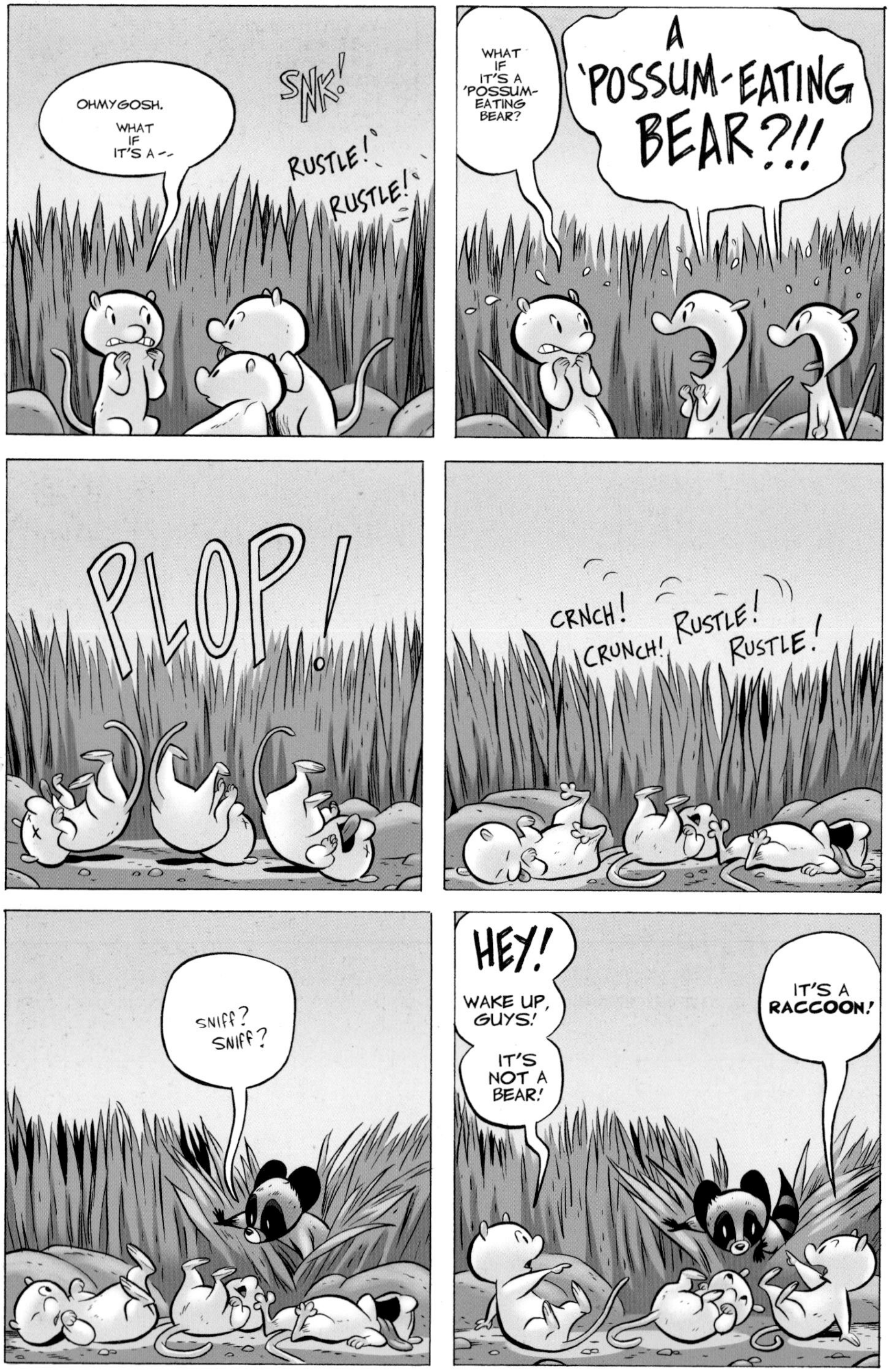
OHMYGOSH. WHAT IF IT'S A--
SNK!
RUSTLE!
RUSTLE!
WHAT IF IT'S A 'POSSUM-EATING BEAR?
A 'POSSUM-EATING BEAR?!!
PLOP!
CRNCH!
CRUNCH!
RUSTLE!
RUSTLE!
SNIFF? SNIFF?
HEY!
WAKE UP, GUYS!
IT'S NOT A BEAR!
IT'S A RACCOON!

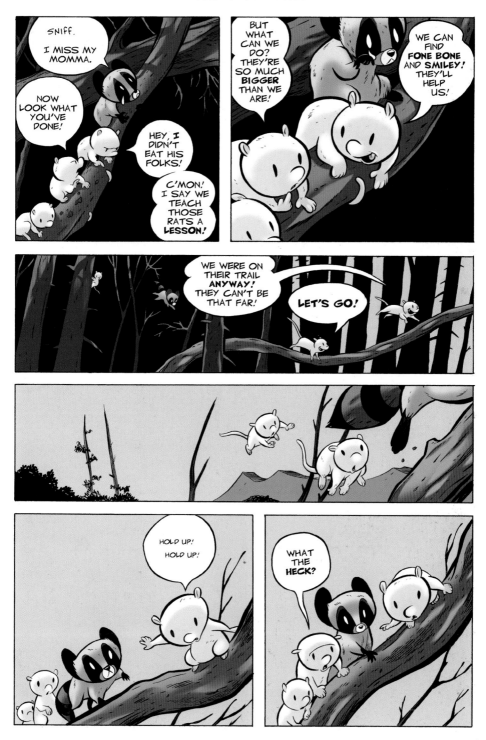

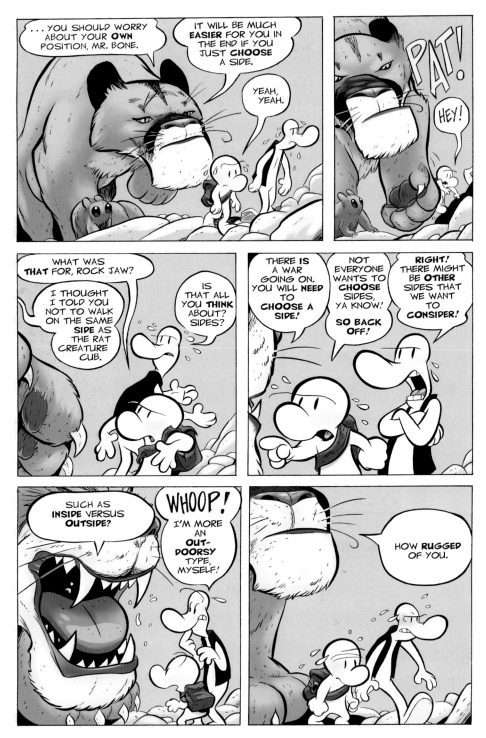

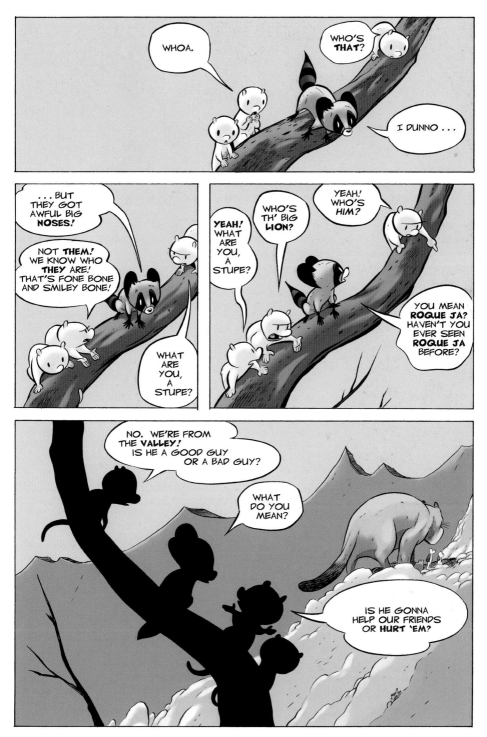

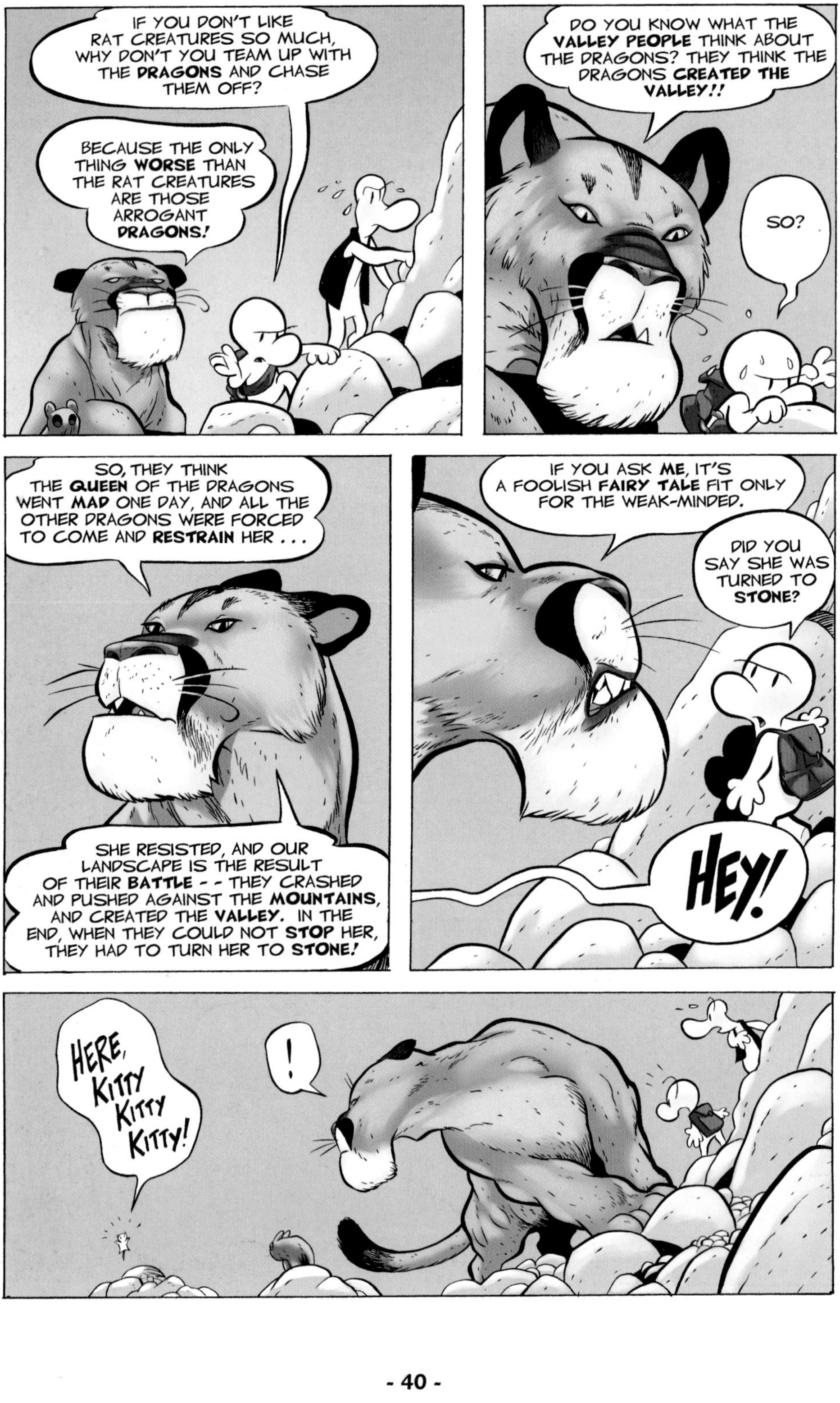
IF YOU DON'T LIKE RAT CREATURES SO MUCH, WHY DON'T YOU TEAM UP WITH THE DRAGONS AND CHASE THEM OFF?
BECAUSE THE ONLY THING WORSE THAN THE RAT CREATURES ARE THOSE ARROGANT DRAGONS!
DO YOU KNOW WHAT THE VALLEY PEOPLE THINK ABOUT THE DRAGONS? THEY THINK THE DRAGONS CREATED THE VALLEY!!
SO?
SO, THEY THINK THE QUEEN OF THE DRAGONS WENT MAD ONE DAY, AND ALL THE OTHER DRAGONS WERE FORCED TO COME AND RESTRAIN HER . . .
SHE RESISTED, AND OUR LANDSCAPE IS THE RESULT OF THEIR BATTLE - - THEY CRASHED AND PUSHED AGAINST THE MOUNTAINS, AND CREATED THE VALLEY. IN THE END, WHEN THEY COULD NOT STOP HER, THEY HAD TO TURN HER TO STONE!
IF YOU ASK ME, IT'S A FOOLISH FAIRY TALE FIT ONLY FOR THE WEAK-MINDED.
DID YOU SAY SHE WAS TURNED TO STONE?
HEY!
HERE, KITTY KITTY KITTY!
!

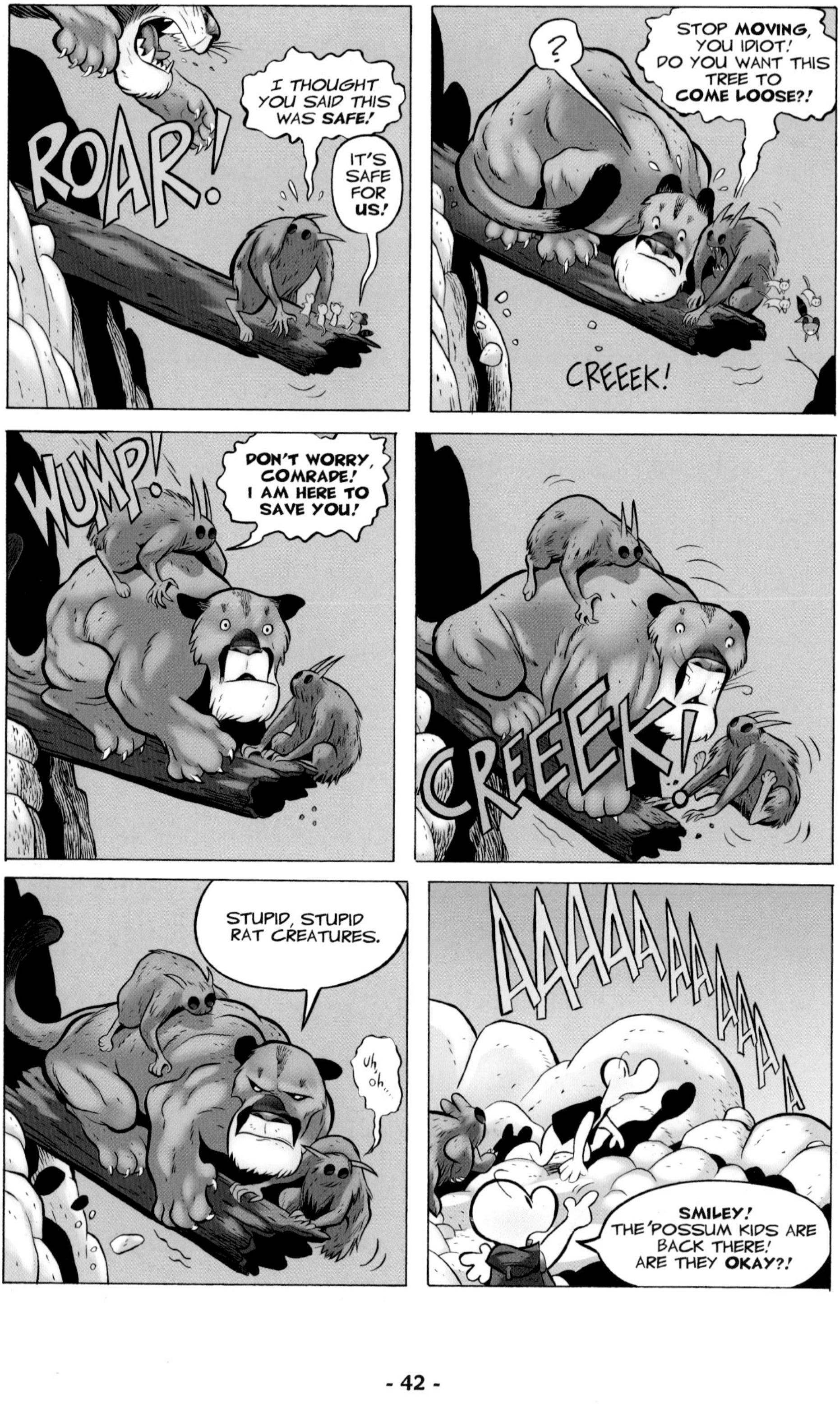
I THOUGHT YOU SAID THIS WAS SAFE!
ROAR!
IT'S SAFE FOR US!
?
STOP MOVING, YOU IDIOT! DO YOU WANT THIS TREE TO COME LOOSE?!
CREEEK!
WUMP!
DON'T WORRY, COMRADE! I AM HERE TO SAVE YOU!
CREEEK!
STUPID, STUPID RAT CREATURES.
uh, oh...
AAAAAAAAAAAAAAA
SMILEY! THE 'POSSUM KIDS ARE BACK THERE! ARE THEY OKAY?!

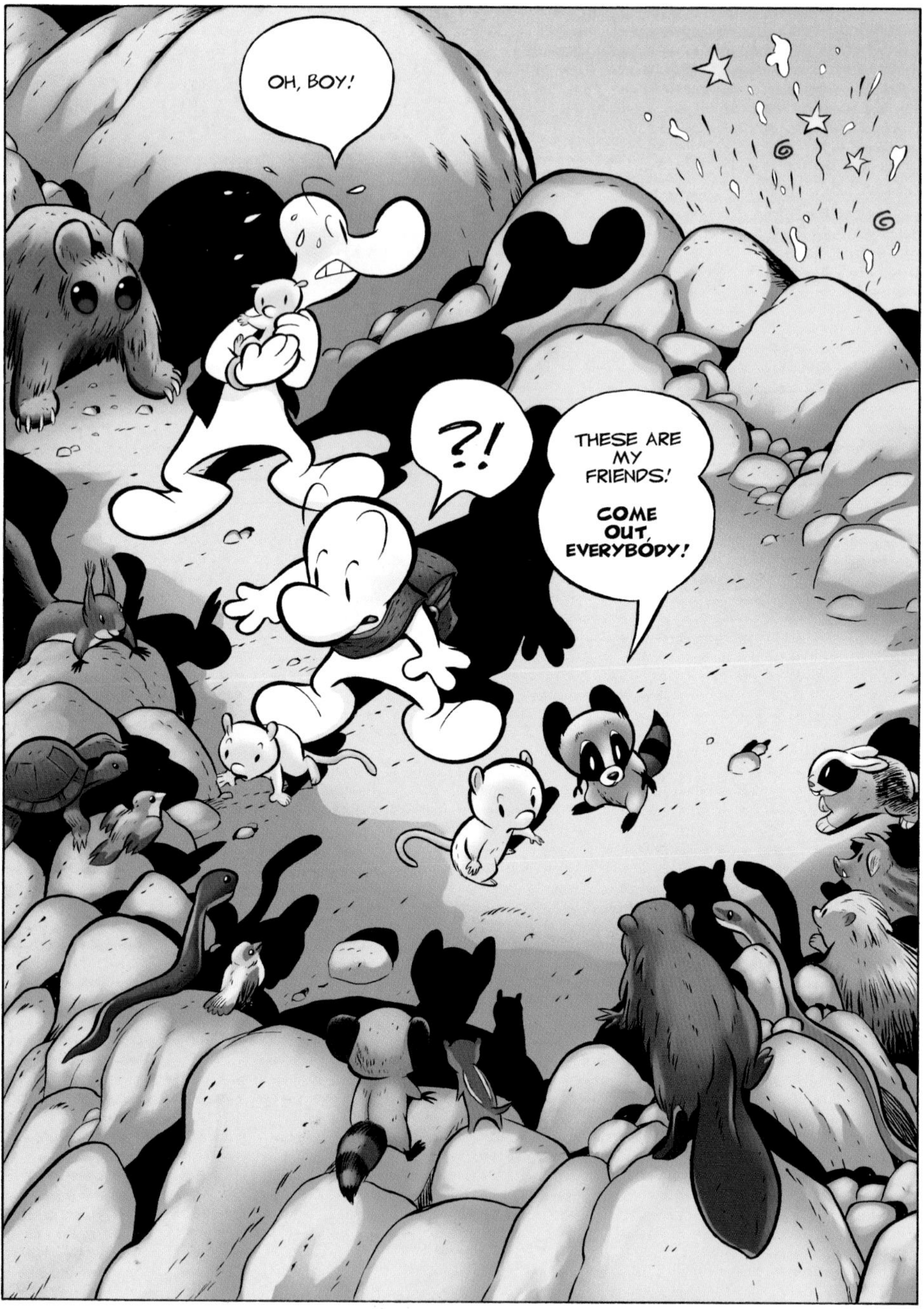
OH, BOY!
?!
THESE ARE MY FRIENDS!
COME OUT, EVERYBODY!

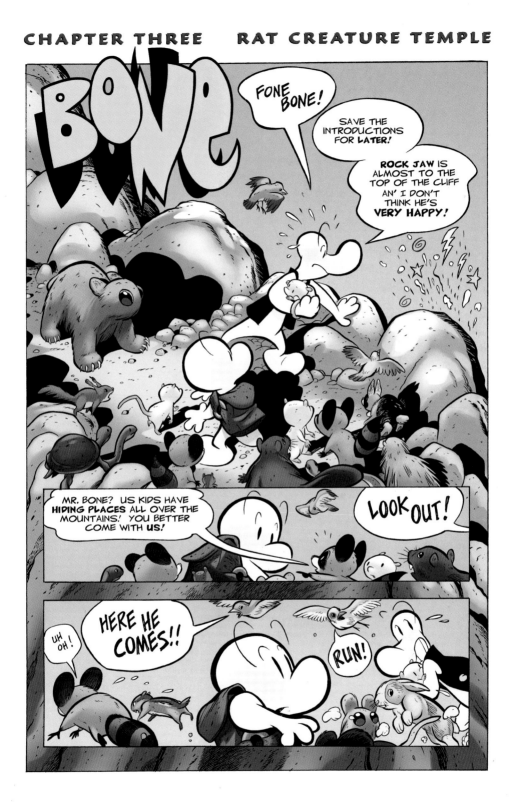

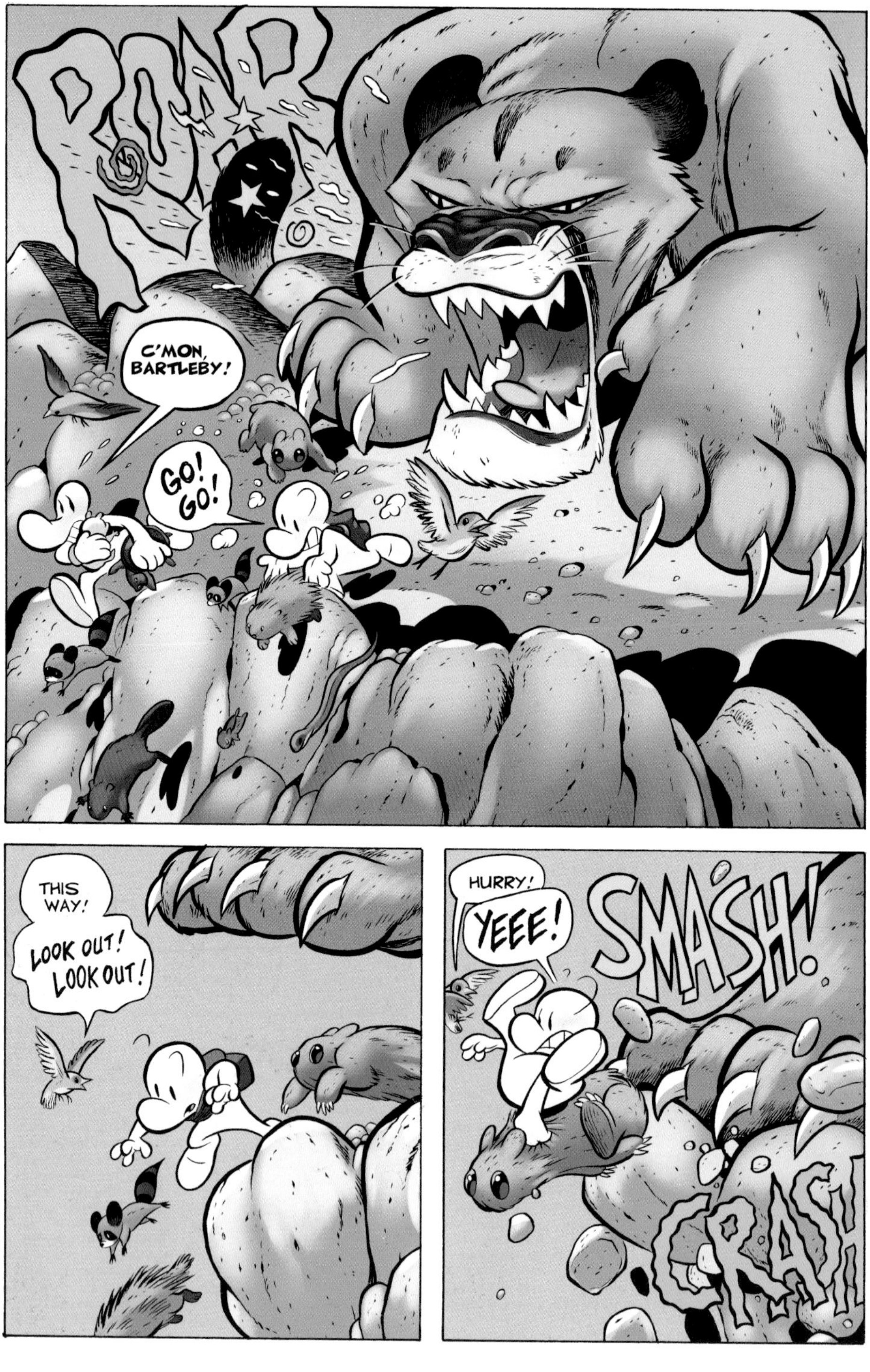
ROAR
C'MON, BARTLEBY!
GO! GO!
THIS WAY!
LOOK OUT! LOOK OUT!
HURRY!
YEEE!
SMASH!
CRASH

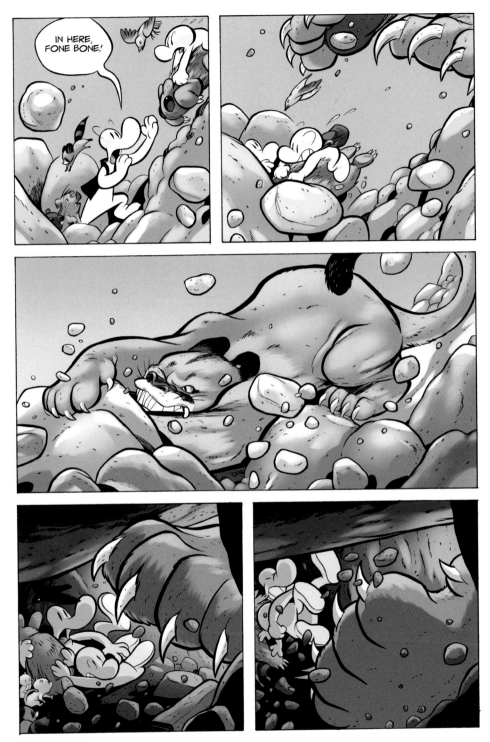

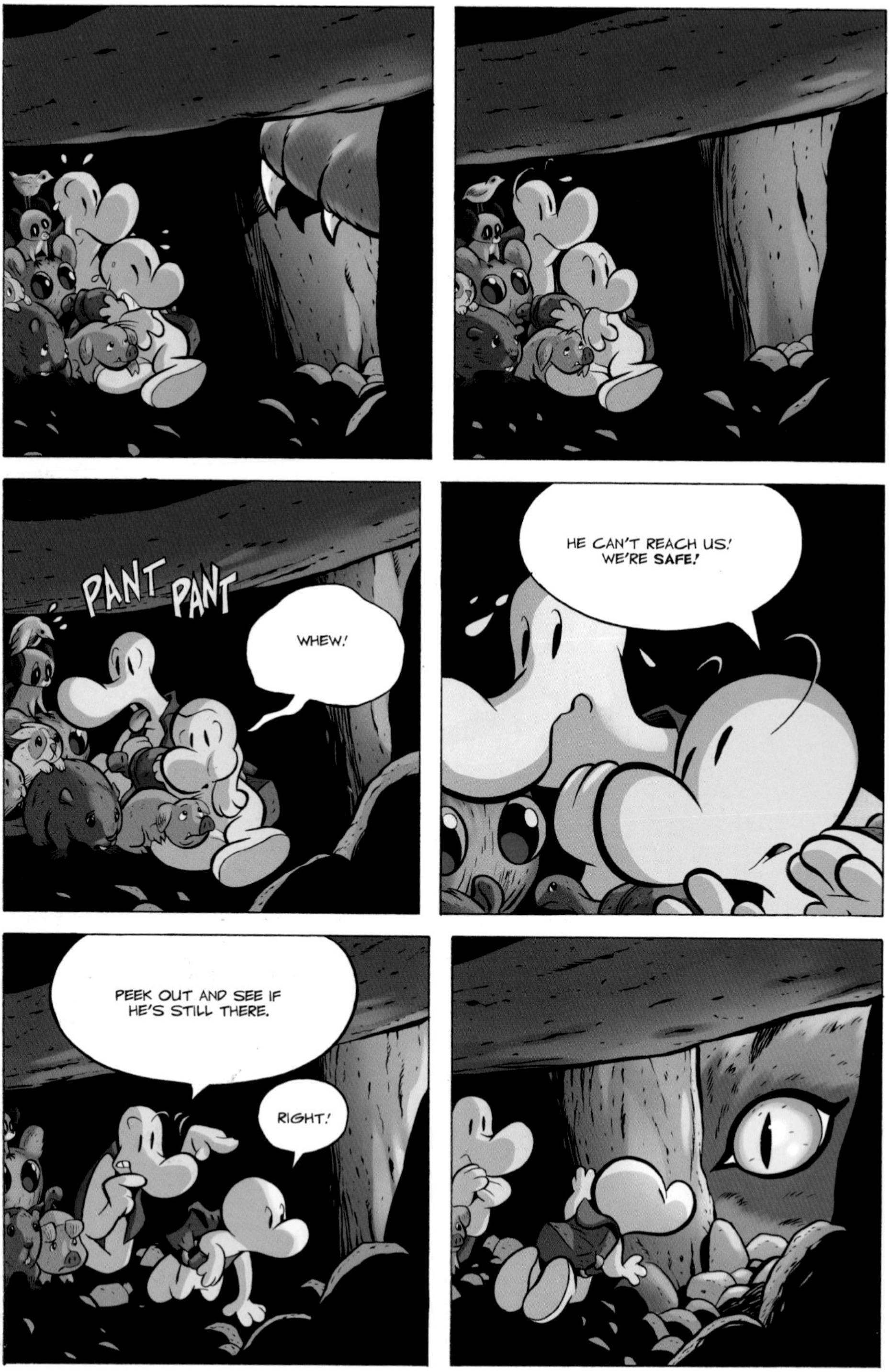
PANT PANT
WHEW!
HE CAN'T REACH US! WE'RE SAFE!
PEEK OUT AND SEE IF HE'S STILL THERE.
RIGHT!

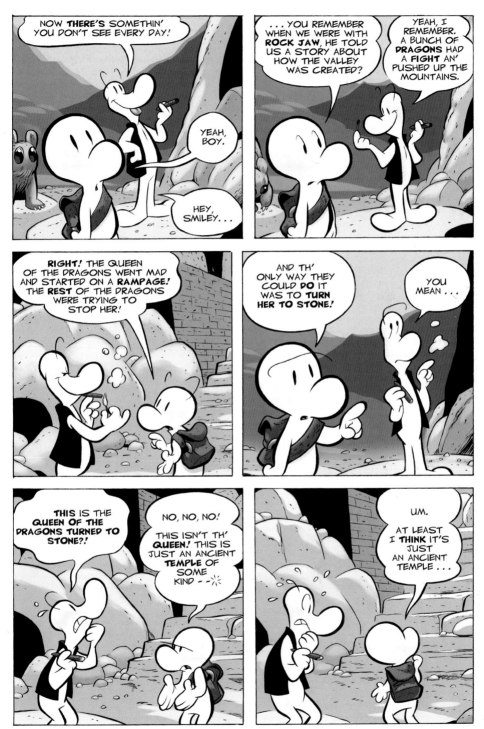

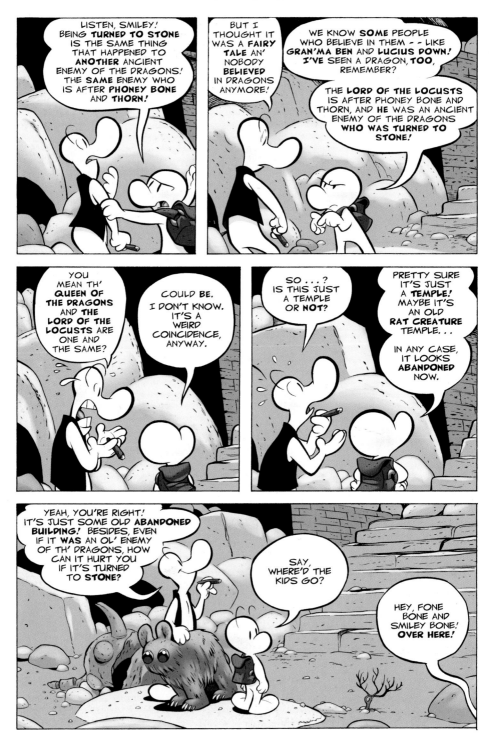

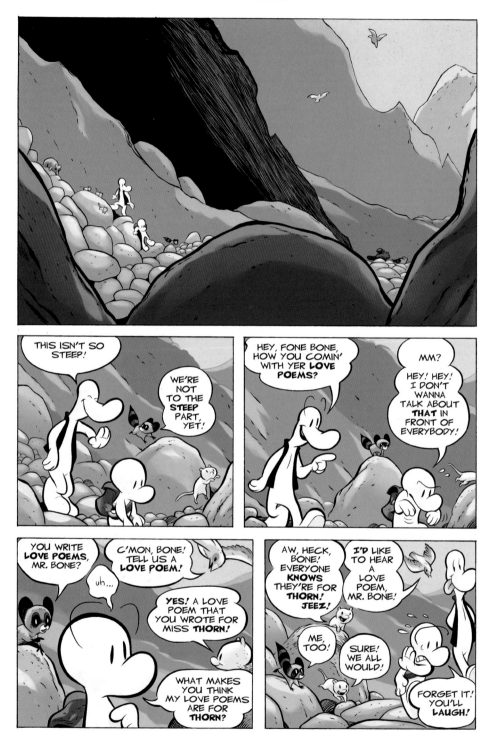

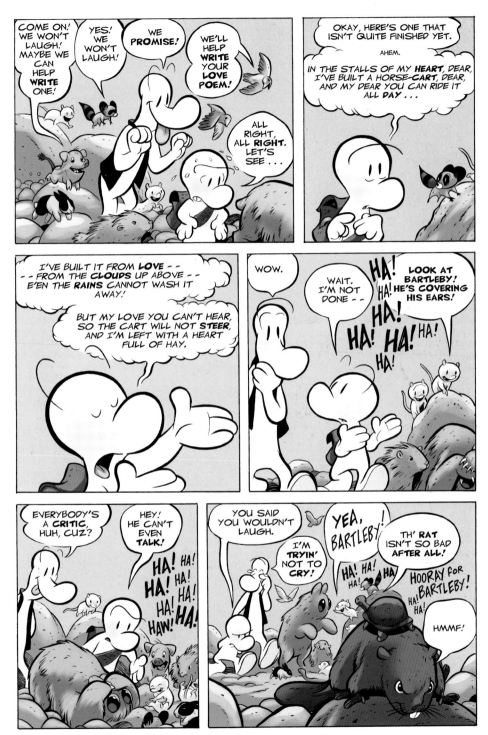

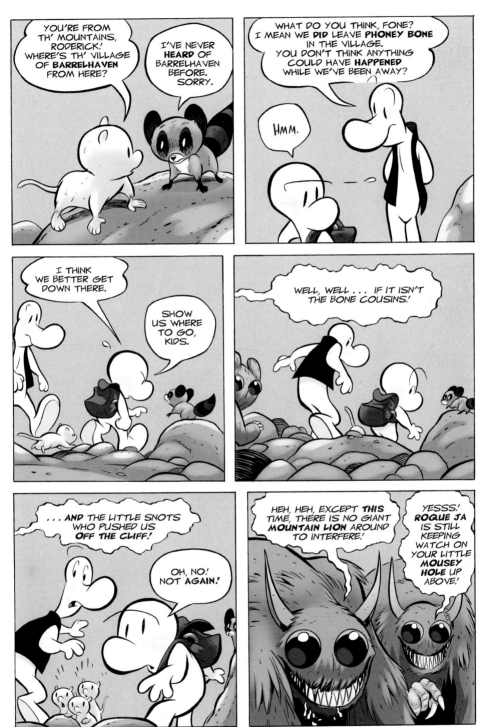

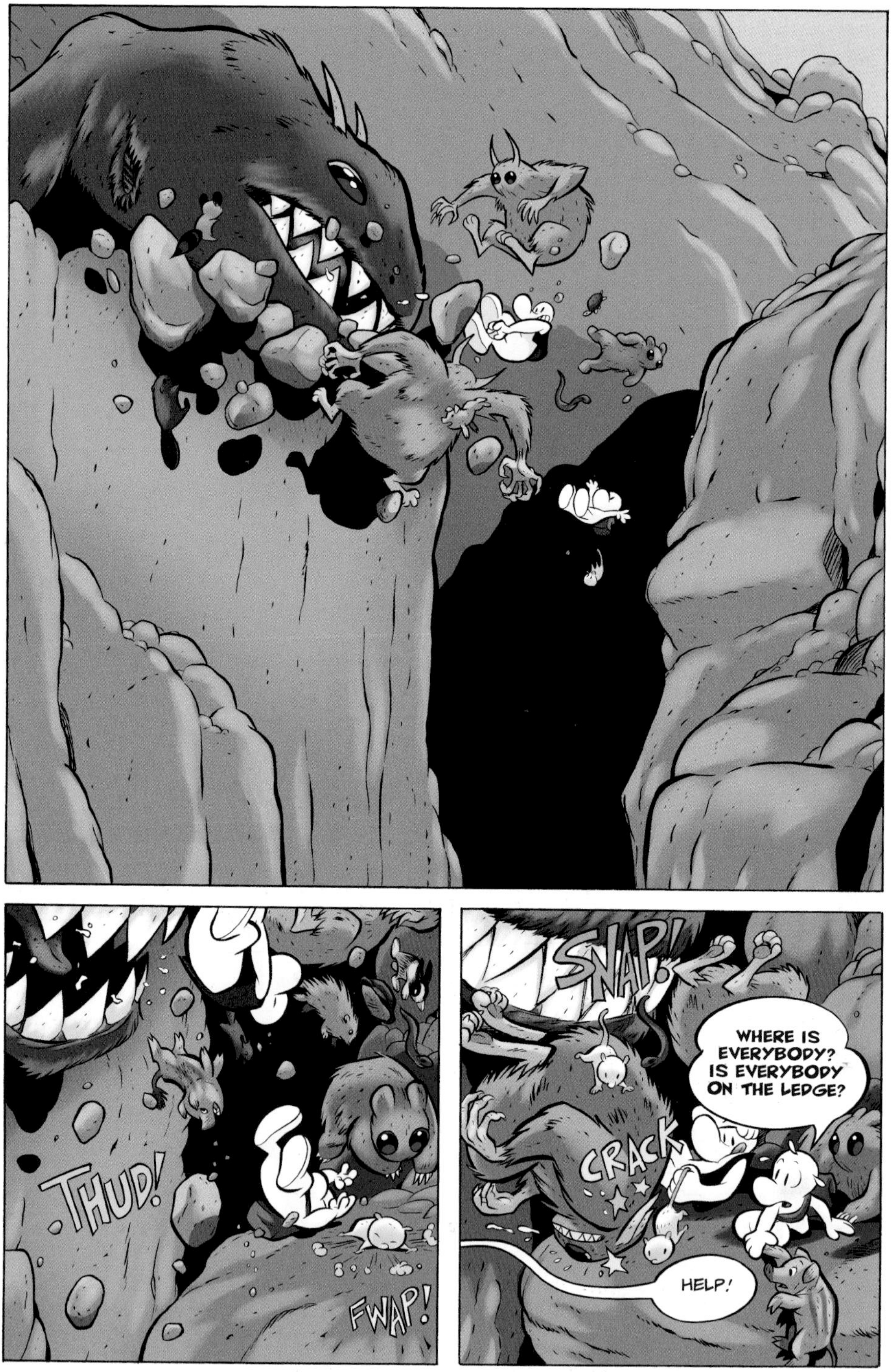
THUD!
FWAP!
SNAP!
WHERE IS EVERYBODY? IS EVERYBODY ON THE LEDGE?
CRACK
HELP!

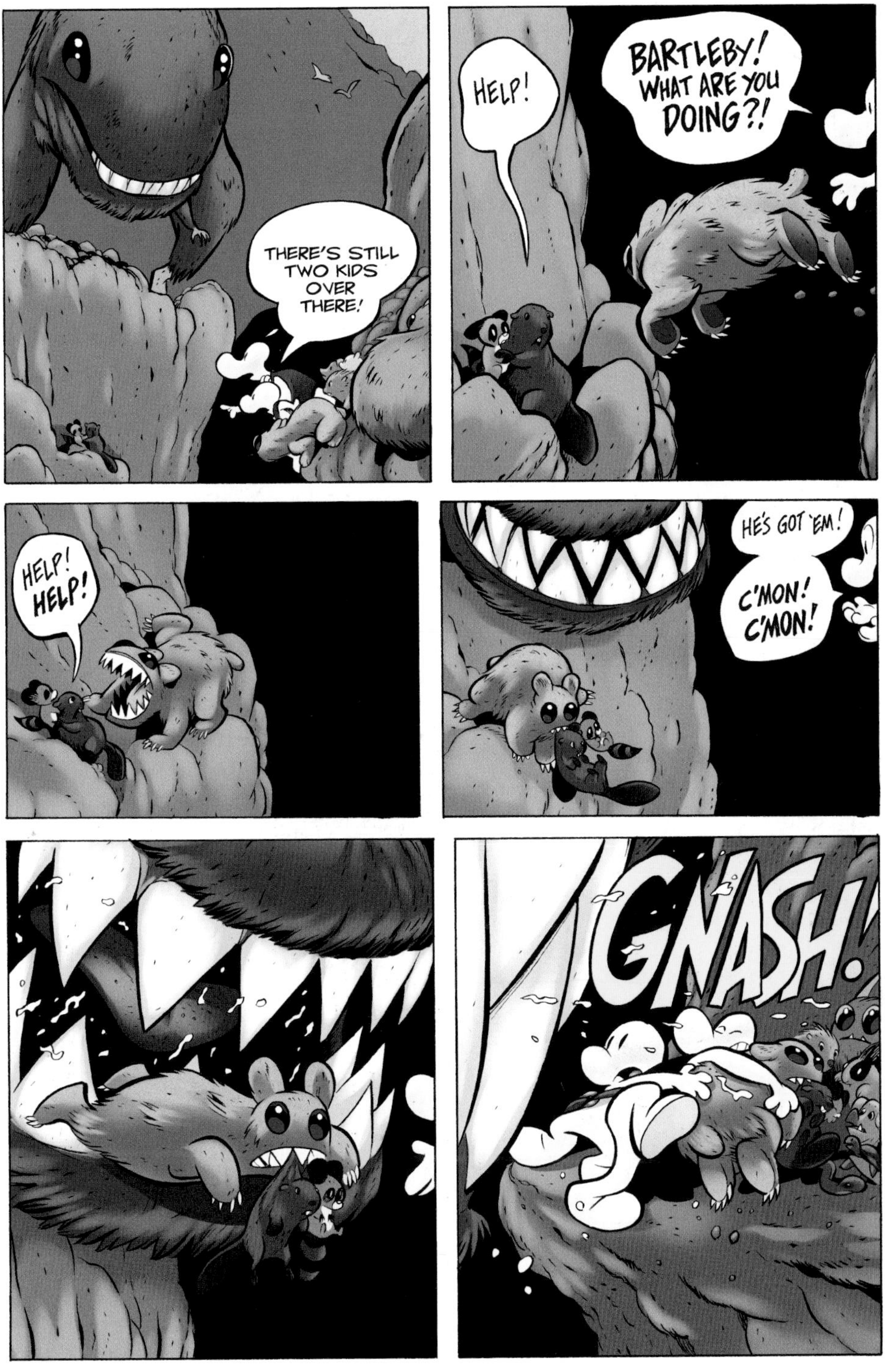
THERE'S STILL TWO KIDS OVER THERE!
HELP!
BARTLEBY! WHAT ARE YOU DOING?!
HELP! HELP!
HE'S GOT 'EM!
C'MON! C'MON!
GNASH!

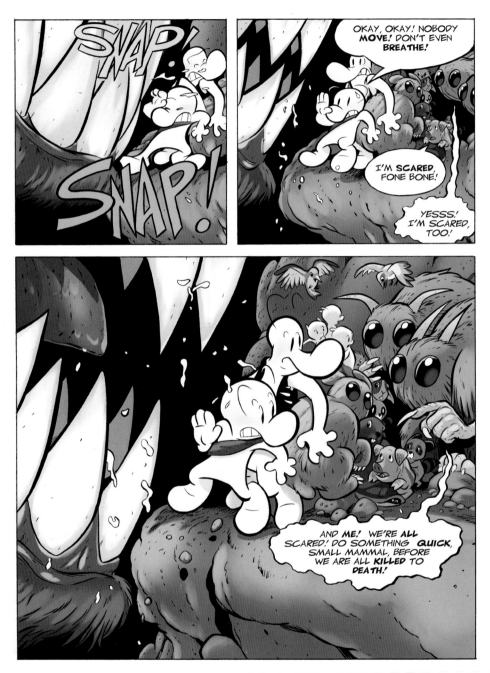

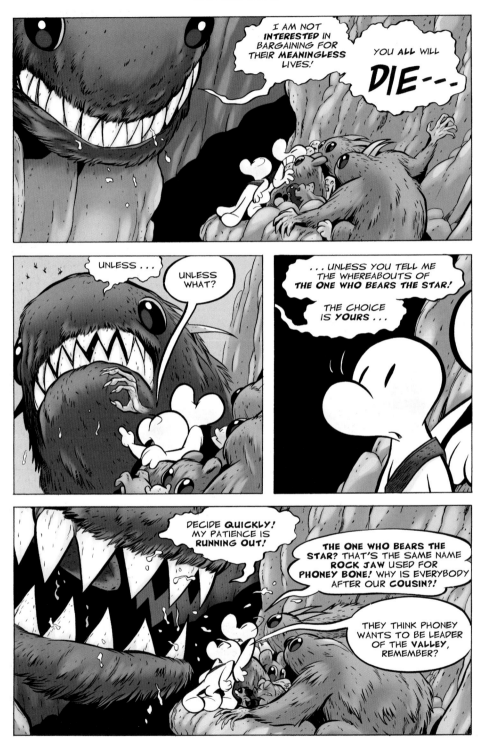

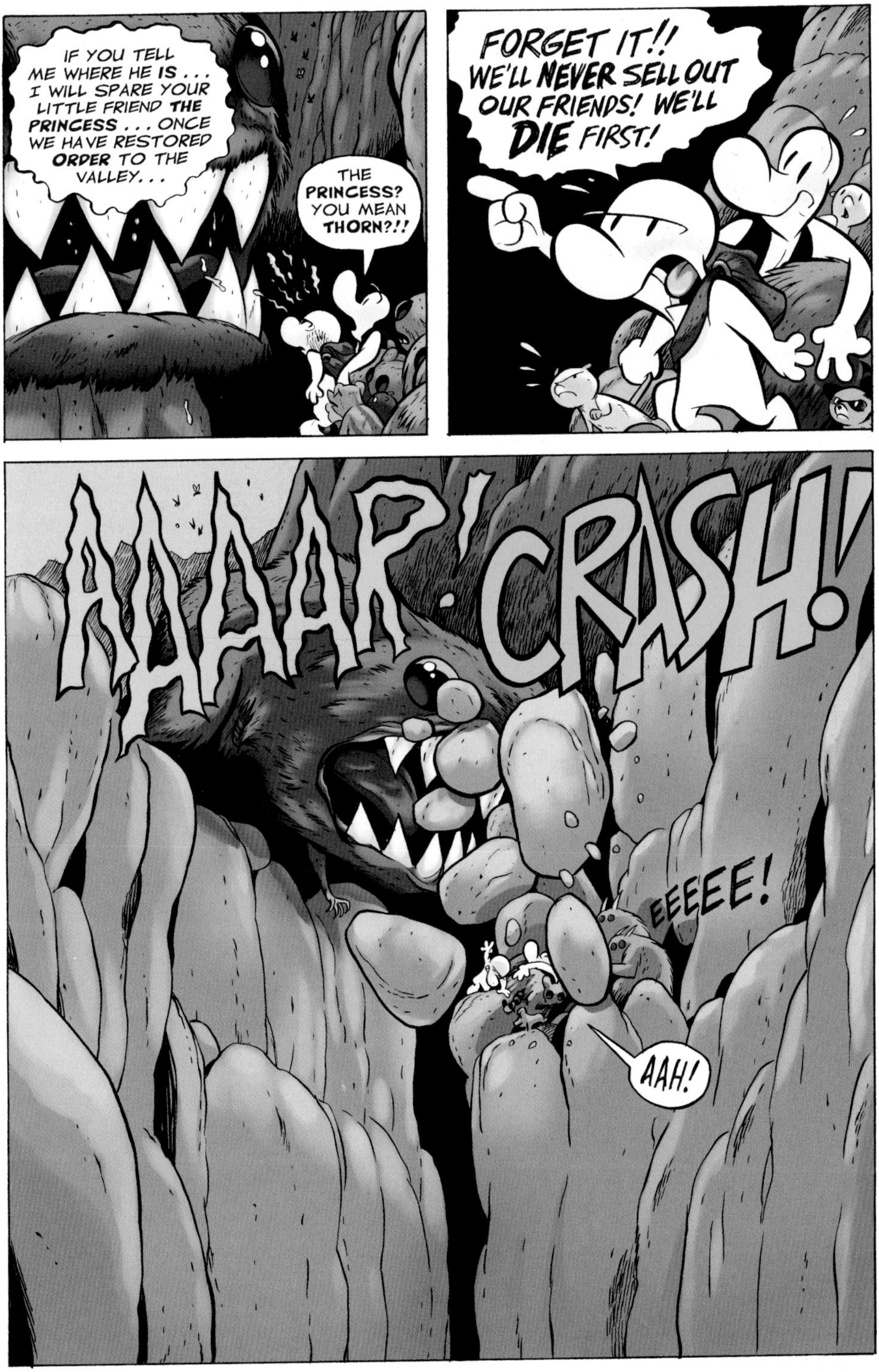
IF YOU TELL ME WHERE HE IS . . . I WILL SPARE YOUR LITTLE FRIEND THE PRINCESS . . . ONCE WE HAVE RESTORED ORDER TO THE VALLEY. . .
THE PRINCESS? YOU MEAN THORN?!!
FORGET IT!! WE'LL NEVER SELL OUT OUR FRIENDS! WE'LL DIE FIRST!
AAAAR!
CRASH!
EEEEE!
AAH!

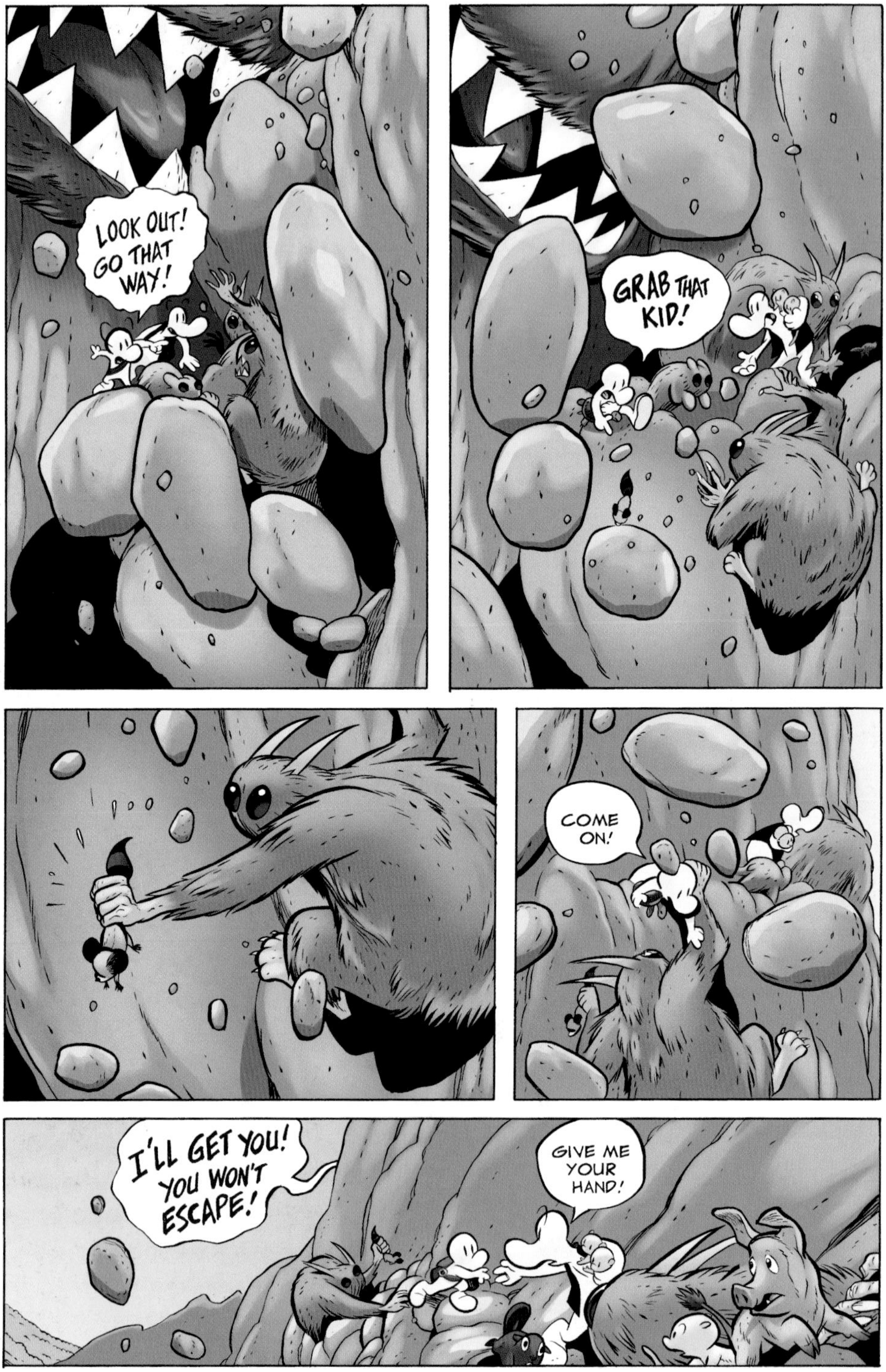
LOOK OUT! GO THAT WAY!
GRAB THAT KID!
COME ON!
I'LL GET YOU! YOU WON'T ESCAPE!
GIVE ME YOUR HAND!

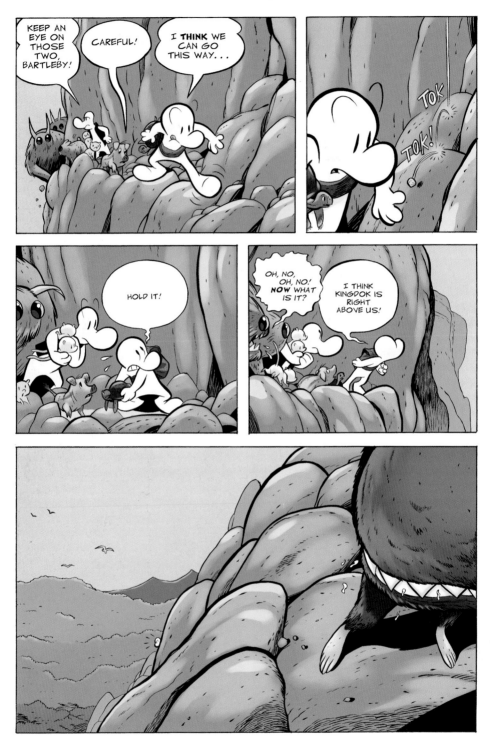

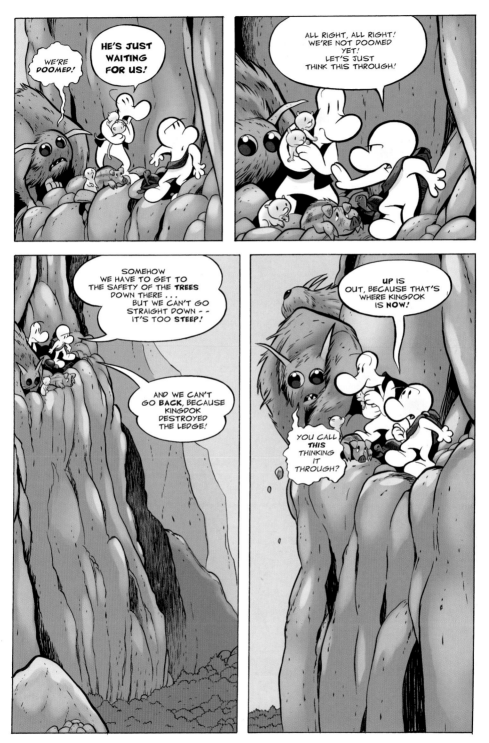

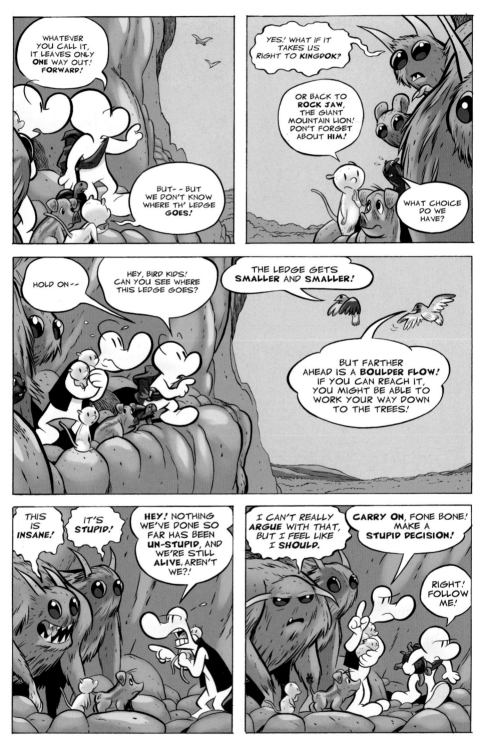

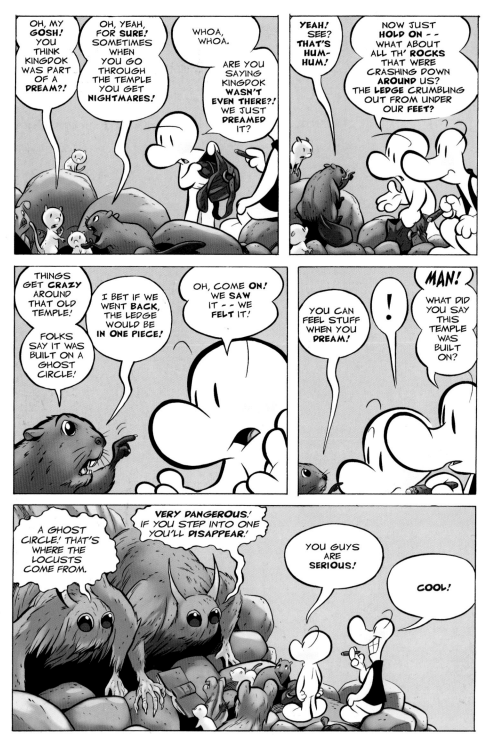

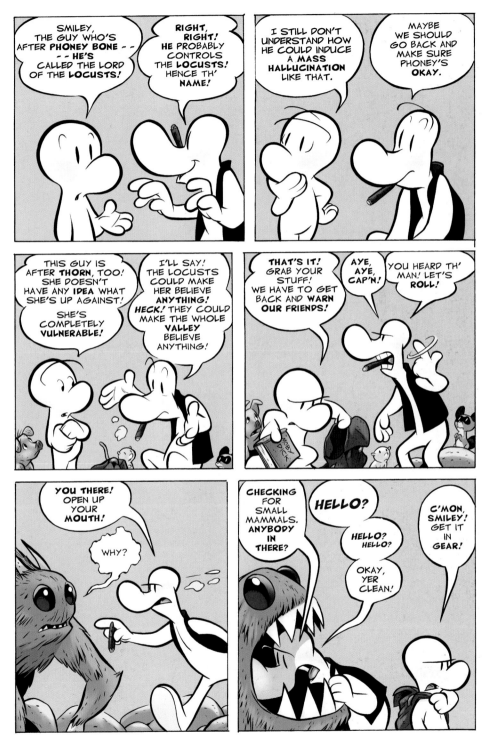

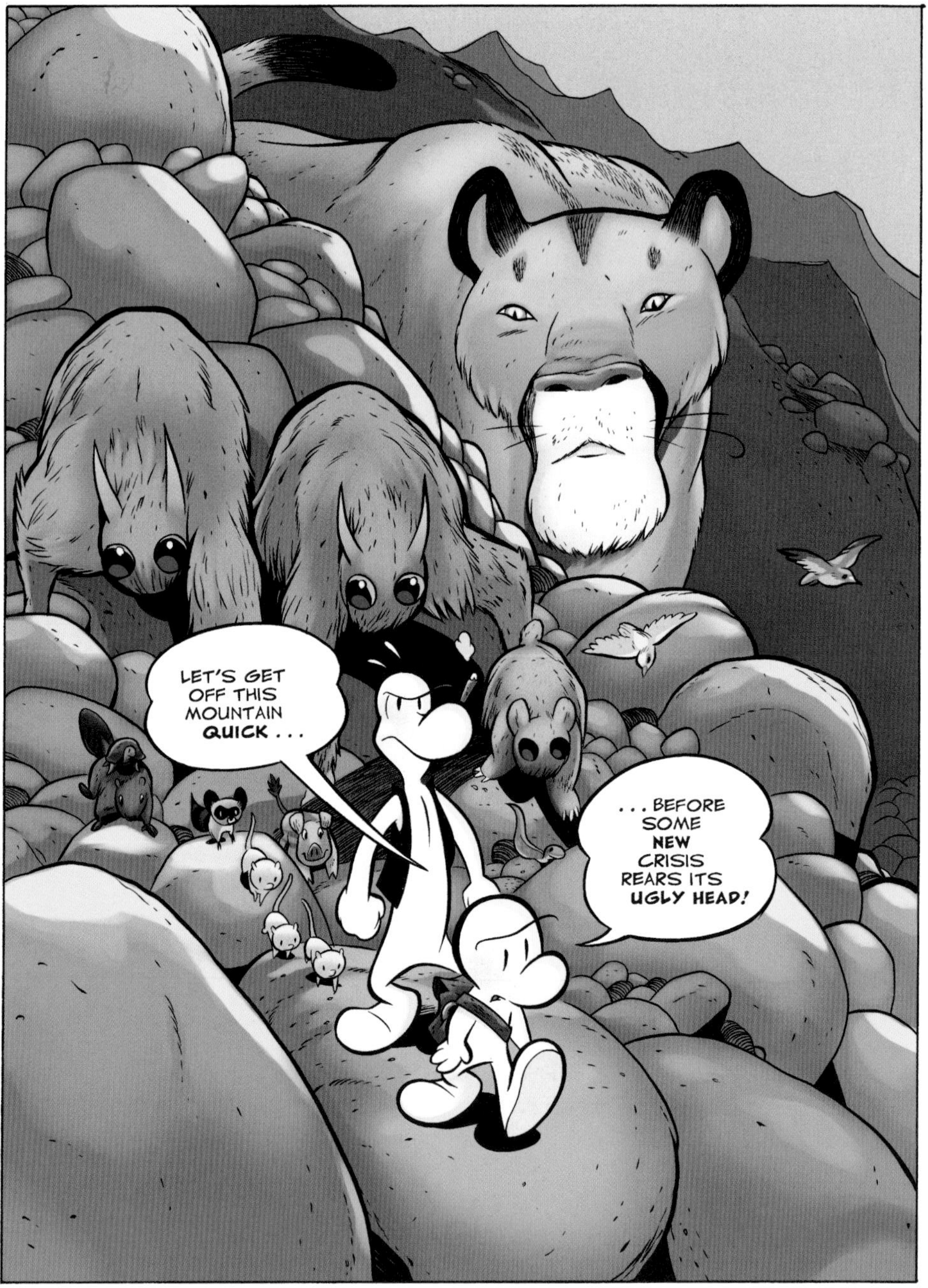
LET'S GET OFF THIS MOUNTAIN QUICK . . .
. . . BEFORE SOME NEW CRISIS REARS ITS UGLY HEAD!

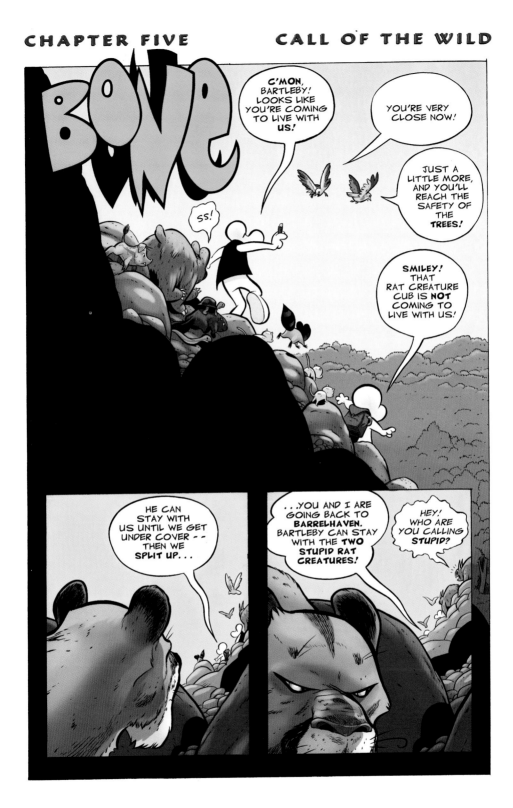

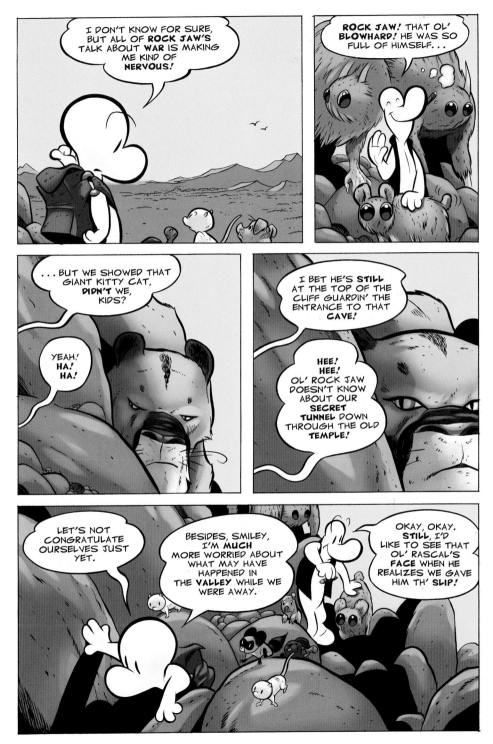

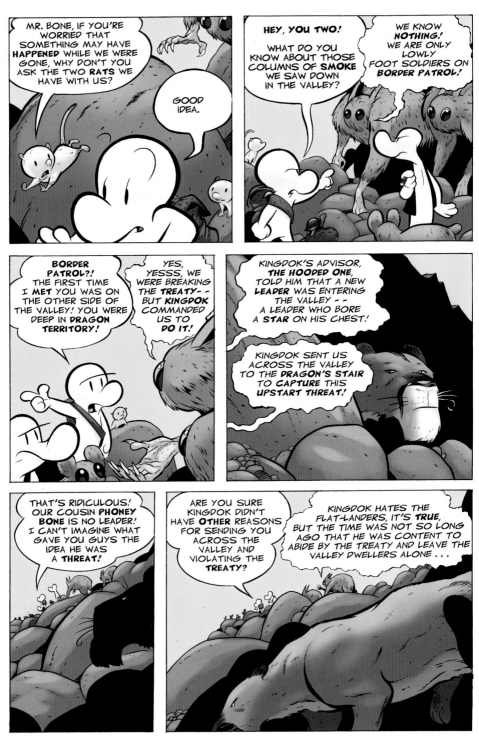

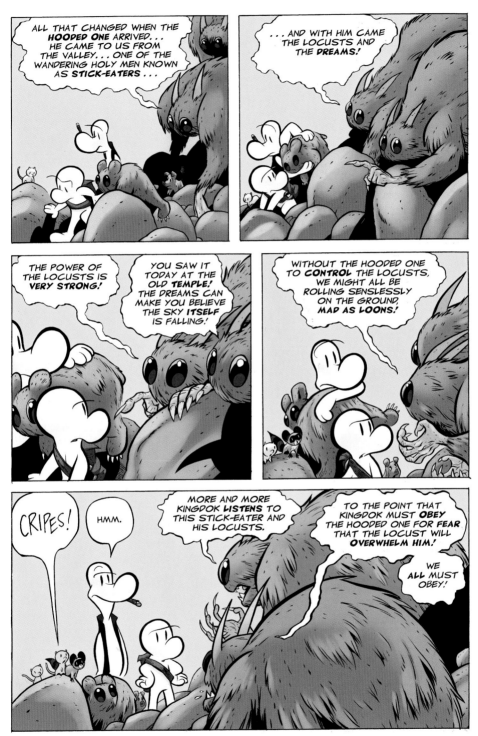

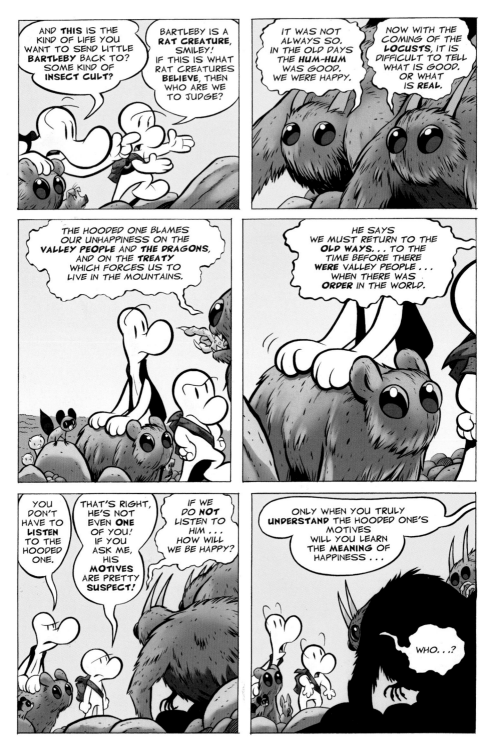

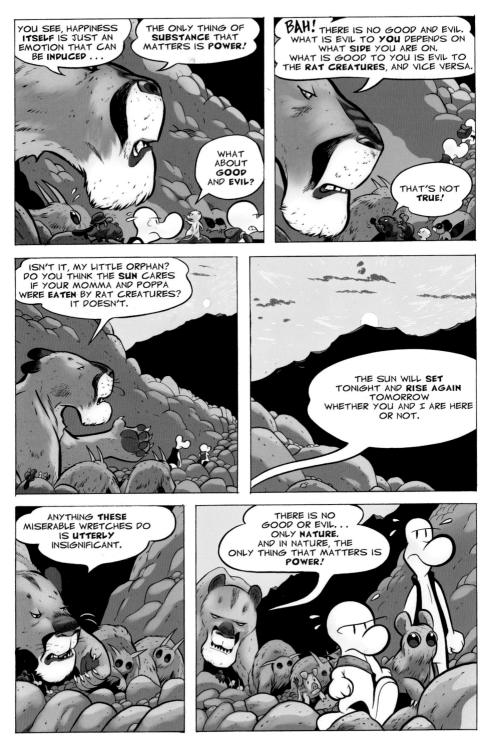

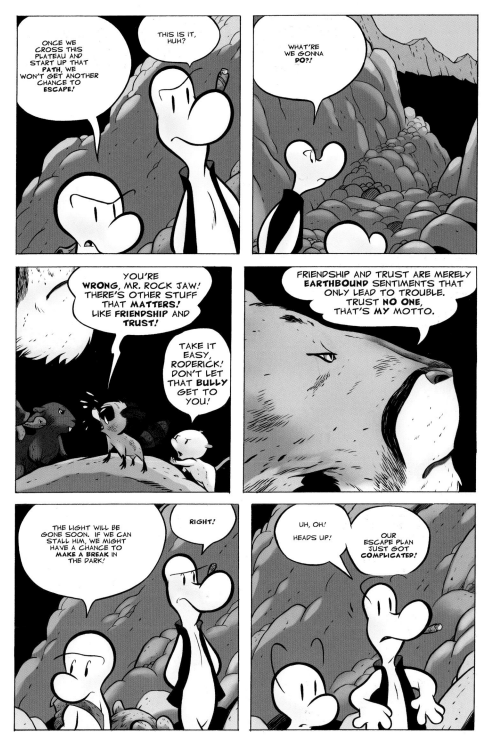

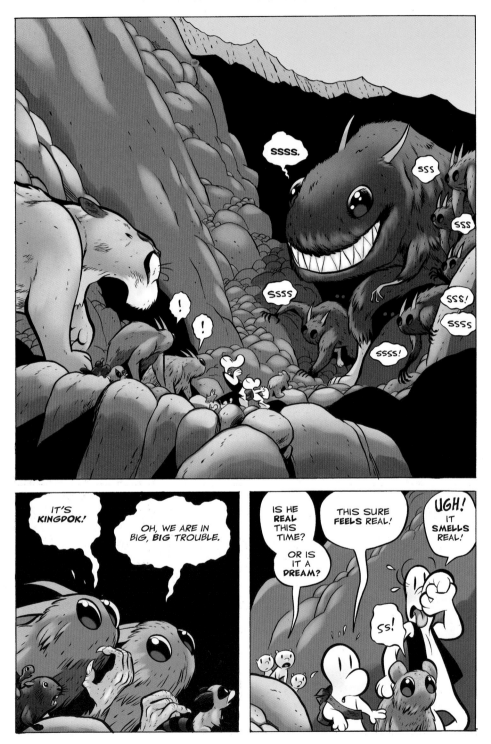

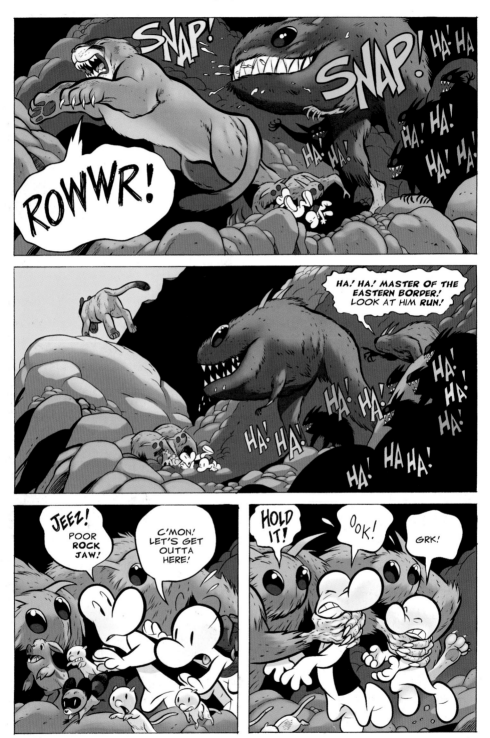

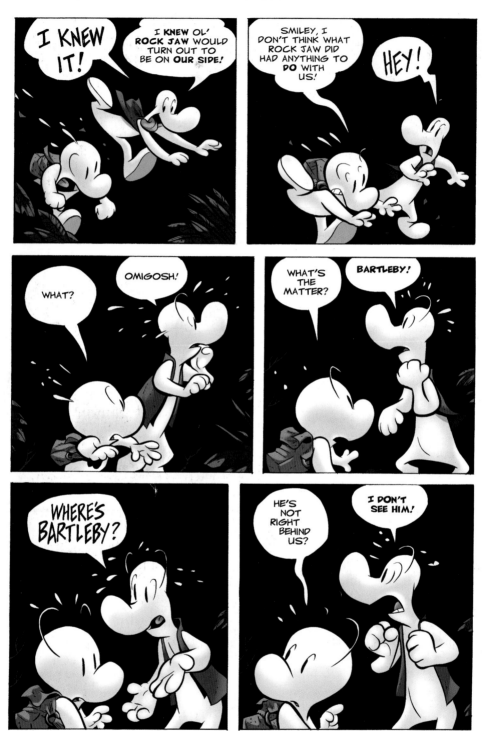

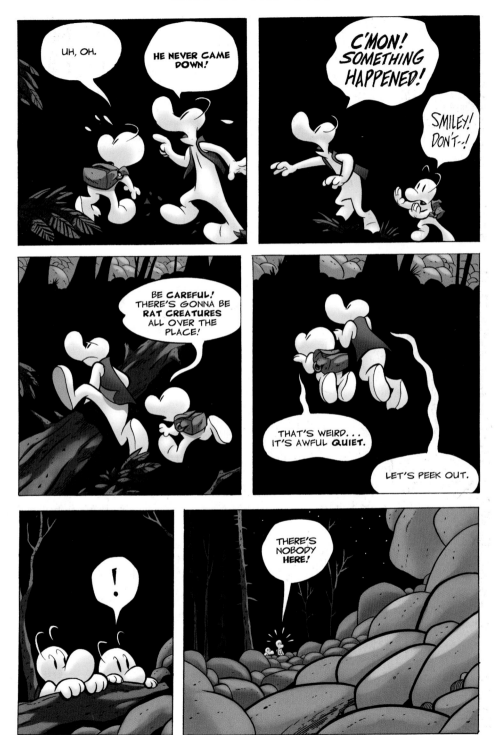

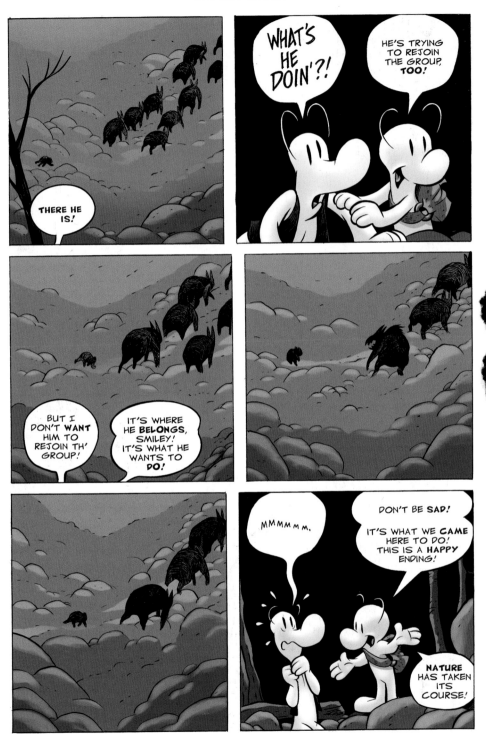

WILL HE BE OKAY?

YEAH. YEAH. HE'LL BE FINE.

LISTEN . . .

YOU CAN WATCH HIM FOR A WHILE IF YOU WANT, BUT NOT TOO LONG -- WE GOTTA GO, ALL RIGHT?

I GUESS.

GOOD-BYE, BARTLEBY.

I GOTTA GO NOW.

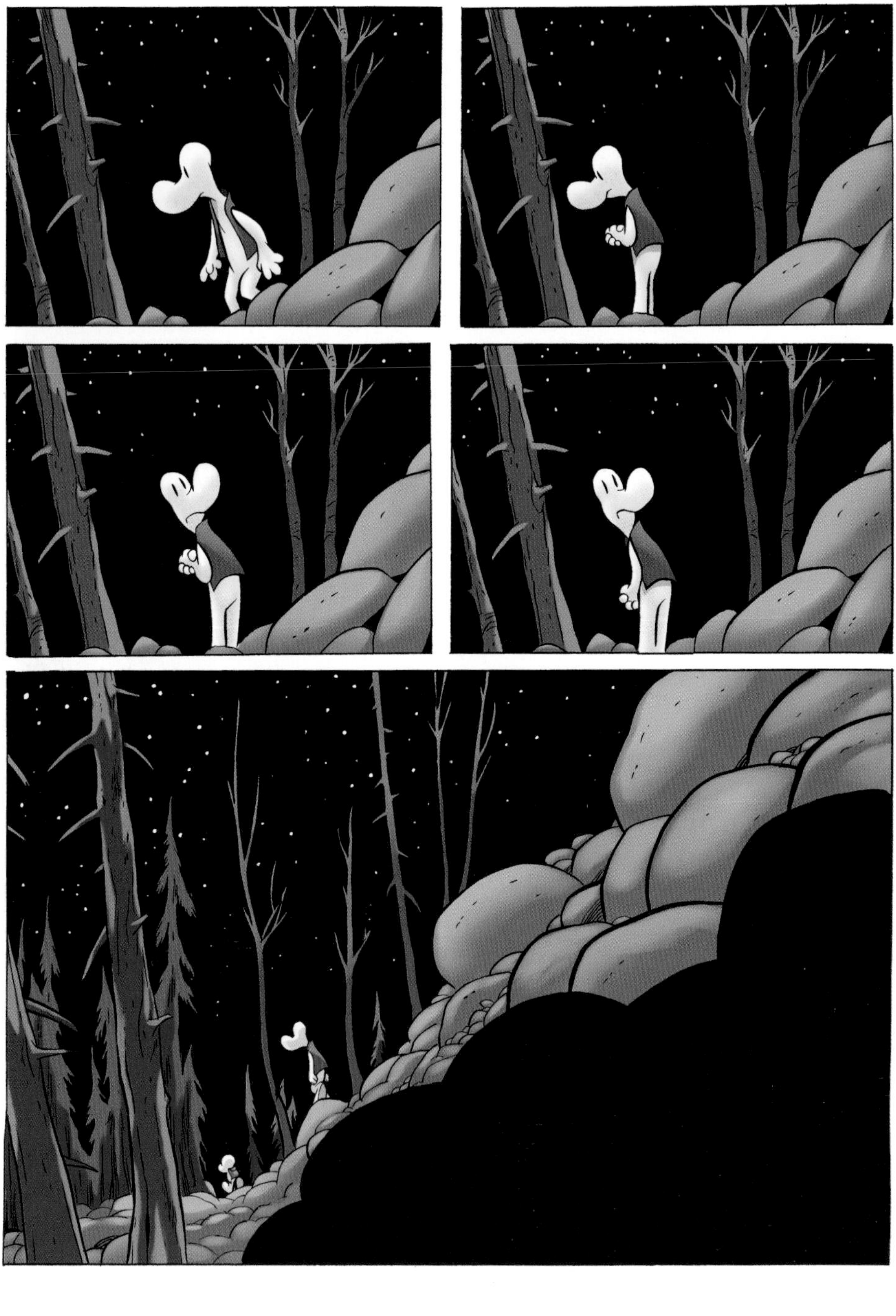

...TO BE CONTINUED.

About JEFF SMITH

JEFF SMITH was born and raised in the American Midwest and learned about cartooning from comic strips, comic books, and watching animated shorts on TV. After four years of drawing comic strips for The Ohio State University's student newspaper and co-founding Character Builders animation studio in 1986, Smith launched the comic book *BONE* in 1991. Between *BONE* and other comics projects, Smith spends much of his time on the international guest circuit promoting comics and the art of graphic novels.

More about BONE

An instant classic when it first appeared in the U.S. as an underground comic book in 1991, Bone has since garnered 38 international awards and sold a million copies in 15 languages. Now, Scholastic's GRAPHIX imprint is publishing full-color graphic novel editions of the nine-book *BONE* series. Look for the continuing adventures of the Bone cousins in *Old Man's Cave*.